The Princess and the Pink Dragon

Thomas Kirschner

Illustrated by Jennifer Gardner

Amazing Things Press

Book design by Julie L. Casey

ISBN 978-0692385739

Printed in the United States of America.

For more information, visit

www.thomaskirschner.weebly.com

or

www.amazingthingspress.com

For the real princess, Delaney Rae McQuiston.

Long Long Ago
In A Place Far Away,
Lived A Little Princess.
They Called Her Laney Rae.

If You Listened To The Gum
Drops
Placed Upon The Door,
Counted Moonbeams With The
Fairies,
Then You Knew That She Was
Four.

She Lived In A Raindrop
Way Upon A Hill.
She Lived There With Her
Mom And Dad
And a Butterfly
Named Bill.

She Had Two older Brothers;
She Called Them Izz And Jake.
They Lived Inside The Beach Ball
Just Across The Walking Lake.

One Day The Little Princess
Went To See Wise Guy.
She Climbed Upon Old Bill
And Away The Two Did Fly.

It Was Early In The Morning
When They Headed Towards The Dawn.
She Never Told Her Parents;
No One Knew That She Had Gone.

They Had Been Gone At Least Two Yellows
When The Clouds Began To Cry.
Old Bill Had to Quickly Land
To Keep His Dust
Wings Dry.

They Waited Through Two Browns
And At Least Five More Yellows.
Then The Clock Began To Count
And The Rocks Turned Into Jellos.

The Princess Started Crying.
Now What Would She Do?
No One Knew She Left The Raindrop;
Even Bill Was Feeling Blue.

Then Off In The Distance
Came The Dragon Of
Pink
With One eye Open
And One That would
Wink.

The Princess Got Excited
And Jumped Into The Air.
Pink Dragon Could Return Her—
The Answer To Her Prayer.

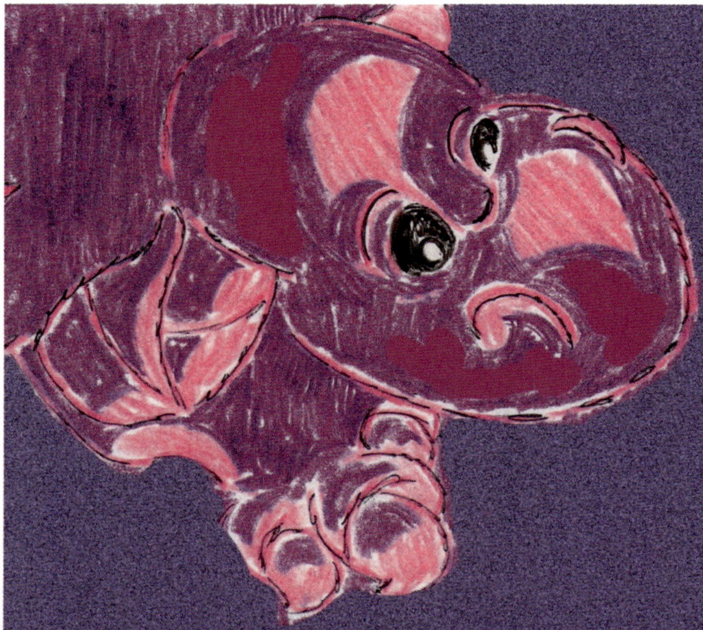

Then The Sky Turned Dark;
It Looked Like It Was Night.
She Worried About Pink Dragon
And Did He Have a Light.

She Heard The Fairies Singing
To Make The Sky Turn Bright.
Then The Sky Lit Up;
Pink Dragon Had A Light.

Pink Dragon Circled Slowly
Then Landed With A Flair.
The Princess And Old Bill
Climbed Up Into The Chair.

They Flew Off Towards Her Raindrop,
Happy As Could Be.
They Passed The Sea Of Worry
And Saw The Purple Tree.

She Saw The Singing Mountains
Covered With Green Snow
She Saw The Walking Lake
And Knew Where She Would Go.

The Beach Ball Moved A Little
When Pink Dragon Settled Down.
She Heard Her Brothers Laughter;
She Knew They Were Around.

She Knew When Mom
And Dad
Called As She Was Late,
She Could Tell Them She
Was Okay,
She's Here With Izz And
Jake.

THE END

About the Illustrator

Jennifer Gardner is a happily married mother of three crazy, wonderful sons. She studied psychology at the University of Kansas and has since pursued a hobby of all things concerning art and raising her children.

Message from the Author

Thank you for taking the time to read my book.
I would be honored if you would
consider leaving a review for it on ***Amazon***.

About the Author

Thomas Kirschner is a 73-year-old retired Architect who wrote poetry for his wife. When she passed away, he continued writing poetry and needed something more to keep from getting bored, so he tried his hand at writing children's books for a hobby.

For more information, please go to:
www.thomaskirschner.weebly.com

Check out these titles from
Amazing Things Press

Keeper of the Mountain by Nshan Erganian

Rare Blood Sect by Robert L. Justus

Evoloving by James Fly

Survival In the Kitchen by Sharon Boyle

Stop Beating the Dead Horse by Julie L. Casey

In Daddy's Hands by Julie L. Casey

Time Lost: Teenage Survivalist II by Julie L. Casey

Starlings by Jeff Foster

MariKay's Rainbow by Marilyn Weimer

Convolutions by Vashti Daise

Seeking the Green Flash by Lanny Daise

Nikki's Heart by Nona j. Moss

Nightmares or Memories by Nona j. Moss

Thought Control by Robert L. Justus

Palightte by James Fly

Check out these children's titles from
Amazing Things Press

The Boy Who Loved the Sky by Donna E. Hart

Terreben by Donna E. Hart

Sherry Strawberry's Clubhouse by Donna E. Hart

Finally Fall by Donna E. Hart

Thankful for Thanksgiving by Donna E. Hart

Make Room for Maggie by Donna E. Hart

Toddler Tales by Kathy Blair

A Cat Named Phyl by Donna E. Hart

Geography Studies With Animal Buddies by Vashti Daise

www.amazingthingspress.com

Made in the USA
Columbia, SC
08 May 2020

96130071R00018